For Lucia

First U.S. edition 2010

Library of Congress Cataloging-in-Publication Data
Docherty, Thomas.
Big scary monster / Thomas Docherty —1st U.S. ed.
p. cm.
Summary: Big Scary Monster learns some surprising things
about himself when he goes down his mountain to find
the creatures he has frightened away.
ISBN 978-0-7636-4787-2
[1. Monsters—Fiction. 2. Self-perception—Fiction. 3. Fear—Fiction.] I. Title.
PZ7.D6618Big 2010
[E]—dc22 2009047397

10 11 12 13 14 15 16 CCP 10 9 8 7 6 5 4 3 2 1

Printed in Shenzhen, Guangdong, China

This book was typeset in Century Schoolbook.
The illustrations were done in watercolor.

TEMPLAR BOOKS

an imprint of
Candlewick Press
99 Dover Street
Somerville, Massachusetts 02144
www.candlewick.com

Thomas Docherty

BIG SCARY MONSTER

templar books
an imprint of Candlewick Press

On top of a mountain, not very far from here, there once lived a Big Scary Monster.

This monster was bigger and scarier than any other creature — and he knew it.

All the other little creatures that lived on the mountain spent their days playing happily together among the small rocks and small plants.

But the Big Scary Monster was never far away, and suddenly, when they least expected it . . .

BOO!

As time went by, the little creatures learned to hide from the Big Scary Monster. He soon got bored because he couldn't find anyone to scare.

One day, as he stood at the top of the mountain and looked down into the valley, he saw many other creatures playing happily in the valley below.

I'll go down there and scare them, he said to himself.

So, off he went down the mountain.

But as he walked, a strange thing happened.

The farther down he got, the larger the things around him appeared to be.

The small rocks . . .

became big rocks.

The small plants . . .

became big plants.

And the little creatures that
had seemed so small from the top of the mountain . . .

were actually very, very big!

The Big Scary Monster had never felt so small and scared in his life.

I wish I was back on the top of the mountain with the little creatures and the small rocks and small plants, thought the Big Scary Monster.

He found a big rock he could hide behind.
Then, suddenly, when he least expected it . . .

BOO!

Back up the mountain ran the Big Scary Monster.

The big plants

became small plants.

The big rocks

became small rocks.

And the little creatures . . .

were nowhere to be found.

The Big Scary Monster felt so alone that he sat down and started to cry.

Then suddenly, when he least expected it . . .

BOO!

The Big Scary Monster was so pleased to see the little creatures that he forgot all about being big and scary.

From that day forward, everyone became friends and played happily together at the top of the mountain. And can you guess what their favorite game was?

BOO!